It Will B

Kasia Reay

Illustrated by Selina Rayner

Schofield & Sims

It is my t<u>ur</u>n. <u>Th</u>is wil<u>l</u> be fun!

L<u>oo</u>k at my <u>c</u><u>ur</u>l. Mmmm.
Let me s<u>ee</u>...

Look! It will be the tail of a pig!
Can you see?

Look at my box. Mmmm.
Let me see...

Look! It will be a big, red bus!
Can you see?

Look at this fur. Mmmm.
Let me see...

I will turn it into a kitten!